**Look at those who are honest
and good, for a wonderful future
awaits those who love peace.**

Psalm 37:37

New Living Translation Bible

MASCOT
KIDS!
an imprint of Amplify Publishing Group

www.mascotbooks.com

Banjo Joe and Mo

For more information, please contact:
Mascot Books, an imprint of Amplify Publishing Group
620 Herndon Parkway, Suite 320
Herndon, VA 20170
info@mascotbooks.com

Library of Congress Control Number: 2022915547

CPSIA Code: PRT1022A
ISBN-13: 978-1-64543-205-0

Printed in the United States

Julia Gonsalves

Illustrated by Matthew Gonsalves

Banjo Joe said, "**Thanky!**" when townsfolk tossed coins into his tin cup.

Sometimes Banjo Joe's **singing** wasn't as good as his **banjo playing.** He sounded like a burro with a bad cold!

The crowd would cheer
"Banjo Joe!" when he began to play.
His biggest fan was **Maureen**, or "Mo" for short.
No one knew which name she fancied
because she had never spoken a word. **Ever.**

SUDDENLY
Mo flung her arms around Banjo Joe's leg
and uttered her first words!

...But he learned to accept Mo's special name for him.

...that no one saw the stranger coming.

seems like there was only room for **ONE** music man in Buckaroo Pass.

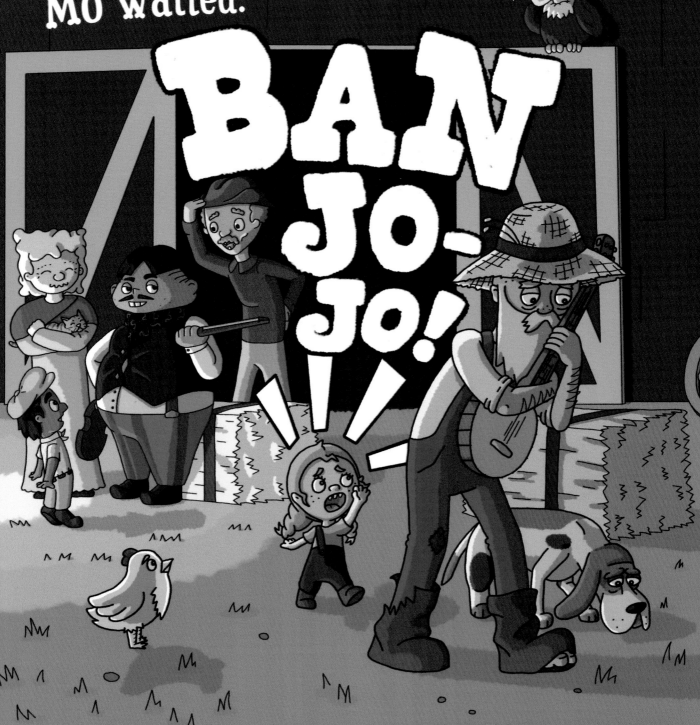

Fiddlin' Pete laughed, "**BAN JO-JO!!!**
That's the **funniest** name I ever did hear!"

Banjo Joe was at a loss for words.

But MO wasn't...

Banjo Joe and Fiddlin' Pete
played together long into the night
for the folks of Buckaroo Pass.

Maybe there **WAS** enough room in
Buckaroo Pass for two music men!

ABOUT THE ILLUSTRATOR

Matthew Gonsalves: Wanted for drawing on the sheriff. (He drew an unflattering mustache.) Witnesses describe him as a lanky and unwashed rapscallion with a goofy disposition. Last seen living under a rock with a bobcat. He is the son of the elusive Julia Gonsalves and may be working with her.

ABOUT THE AUTHOR

Julia Gonsalves: Wanted for disorderly literary conduct. (She engaged in letter rustling of wholesome names.) Witnesses describe her as a reclusive and poufy haired granny. Last seen running with a gang of varmints. She is the mother of Matthew Gonsalves and may be avoiding him. Approach with caution...